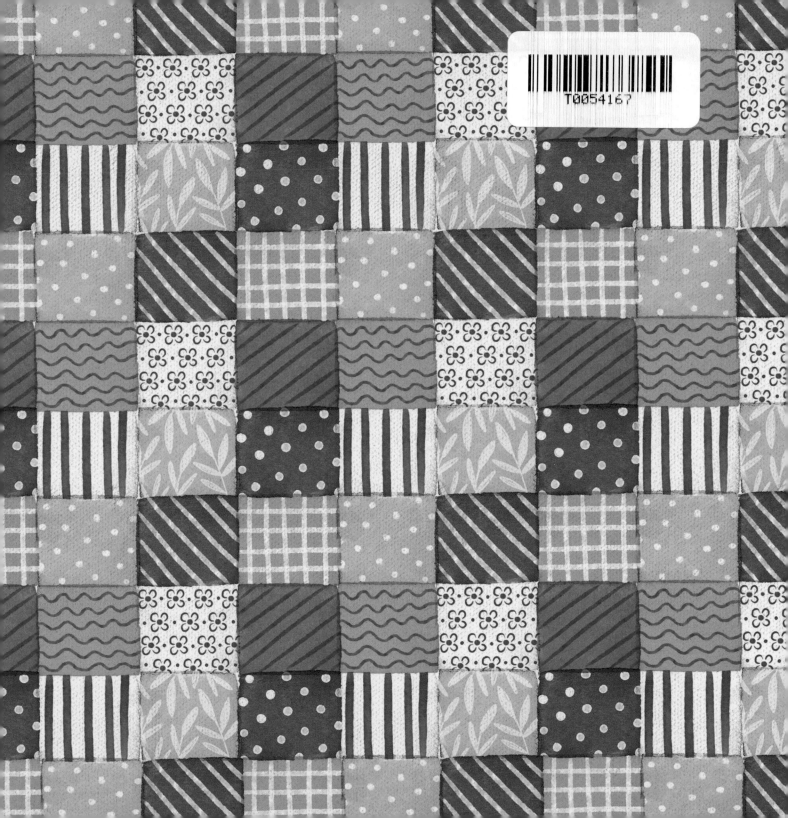

ARLO AND THE GREAT BIG COVER-UP

by Betsy Childs Howard

illustrated by Samara Hardy

CROSSWAY®

WHEATON, ILLINOIS

Library of Congress Cataloging-in-Publication Data

Names: Howard, Betsy Childs, 1981– author. | Hardy, Samara, illustrator.
Title: Arlo and the great big cover-up / Betsy Childs Howard ; illustrations by Samara Hardy.
Description: Wheaton, Illinois : Crossway, [2020] | Summary: "Arlo colors on his wall during naptime, then begins a desperate attempt to hide his disobedience. His mother forgives him. Arlo learns that we cannot hide sin from God, and that confession opens the door to mercy and reconciliation"— Provided by publisher.
Identifiers: LCCN 2019025216 | ISBN 9781433568527 (hardcover)
Subjects: CYAC: Obedience—Fiction. | Honesty—Fiction. | Forgiveness—Fiction. | Parent and child—Fiction. | Christian life—Fiction.
Classification: LCC PZ7.1.H683 Ar 2020 | DDC [E]—dc23
LC record available at https://lccn.loc.gov/2019025216

RRDS			30	29	28	27	26	25	24	
15	14	13	12	11	10	9	8	7	6	5	4	3

"Whoever conceals his transgressions will not prosper,

but he who confesses and forsakes them will obtain mercy."

PROVERBS 28:13

It happened during quiet rest time.

Arlo noticed a scratch on the wall, just over his bed.

The scratch looked like a mouth.

Arlo was not allowed to get off his bed during quiet rest time. But if he kept one foot on his bed and stretched his other leg out, he could reach the markers on his desk.

Then Arlo did a very naughty thing.
He took the cap off the blue marker.

He drew a nose.
And two eyes.

ON THE WALL!

Arlo felt funny. He was not allowed to draw on the walls. Not with a pencil, not with a crayon, and, above all, not with a marker.

Arlo sat on the bed and thought. He took the cap off the brown marker and drew a frame around the face.

He thought the frame might make the face look like it belonged
on the wall. But Arlo's square was not quite square, and he knew
his mom would not be fooled.

Arlo thought some more. He grabbed some tissues from the bedside table and started scrubbing.

It was no use. The marker did not come off the wall, but it did smear together. Arlo had made a big blue and brown mess!

Arlo felt afraid.

His mom was *not* going to be happy with him. He must find a way to cover up the mess on the wall before the end of quiet rest time.

He got off the bed. (This time he didn't bother to keep one foot on.)

He dumped out his toy box, picked it up, and put it on the bed.
It was no good. He could still see the mess on the wall.

He piled up games on top of the box.
The eyes on the wall kept looking at him.

His heart was beating fast.
He grabbed books and toys and piled them higher.

Arlo had done it! The drawing could not be seen behind
the towering pile of toys.

Just then he heard his mom coming up the stairs.
He scrambled under the bed.

"Arlo?" his mom said. "Where are you?"
Arlo kept quiet.

His mom sat down on the bed.

All at once, the tower came tumbling down.

"Arlo," she said, "come out here."

Arlo crawled out from under the bed, but he covered his eyes.
His mom picked him up and put him in her lap.
"Arlo," she said, "Did you color on the wall with a marker?"

Arlo kept his hands over his eyes and shook his head.

His mom pulled his hands away and looked him in the eyes.

"Arlo," she said again, "Did you color on the wall with a marker?"

He looked back at her, and this time he told the truth.

"Yes," he said in a voice that could barely be heard.

"Did you cover it up?"

Arlo took a deep breath.

"Yes," he said (a little louder this time).

"Arlo," she said, "You disobeyed when you colored on the wall.
You also disobeyed when you got off your bed to get your toys."
Arlo threw his arms around his mother. "I'm sorry!
I'm sorry I disobeyed!"

Arlo's mother gave him a tight squeeze. "I forgive you, Arlo."

"Am I going to get a punishment?" he asked without letting go.

"Yes. You have lost your screen time for today and tomorrow."

Arlo felt a little sad. He liked to watch a video while he ate his afternoon snack. But he couldn't feel *too* sad while his mom was hugging him.

Then Arlo had a thought. He sat up and, with a worried voice, asked,
"Will I always have this mess over my bed?"

Arlo's mom smiled. "I thought I would get my super sponge out from under the sink and clean it off. Would you like that?"

"Oh, yes!" Arlo said.

As they walked downstairs to get the sponge, Arlo's mom said, "You know, sometimes when I do something wrong, I want to hide."

Surprised, Arlo asked, "You do? Who do you hide from?"

"When I sin, I want to hide it from God. I don't want him to know about it, and I don't want to talk to him because he might find out."

"That's silly!" Arlo said. "God knows everything already."

"I know!" said his mom. "We *can't* hide our sin from God, and when we try, it only makes us unhappy."

Arlo thought for a minute. "I was unhappy when I was hiding from you under the bed."

"I know," said his mom. "And I knew that you would never be able to get the mess off the wall without my help. I'm glad you came out and told the truth. When we tell God the truth about our sin, he is ready and waiting to help us. That's why he sent his Son Jesus."

Arlo looked at the clean wall. He threw his
arms around his mom again. "Thank you for
washing off my mess," he said. "Cleaned up
is much, much better than covered up."

THE END

Note to Grown-Ups

EVER SINCE THE GARDEN OF EDEN, men and women (and boys and girls) have been trying to hide their sin from God. We instinctively know that sin damages our relationship with our Maker, yet our impulse to hide sin only makes matters worse. The more Arlo tried to cover up his mess, the more miserable he became. In the same way, relief comes to us only when we confess our sins to God and accept his forgiveness. King David describes the transition from the misery of guilt to the joy of forgiveness in Psalm 32.

How do we know God will offer us forgiveness the way Arlo's mom did? We have these promises from God's word:

> But if we walk in the light, as he is in the light, we have fellowship with one another, and the blood of Jesus his Son cleanses us from all sin. If we say we have no sin, we deceive ourselves, and the truth is not in us. If we confess our sins, he is faithful and just to forgive us our sins and to cleanse us from all unrighteousness. (1 John 1:7–9)

We hope that children will remember Arlo's story when they disobey and are tempted to cover up their sins. It is never too early to learn to come out of hiding and into the light, where the blood of Jesus cleanses us and our loving Father welcomes us into his arms!

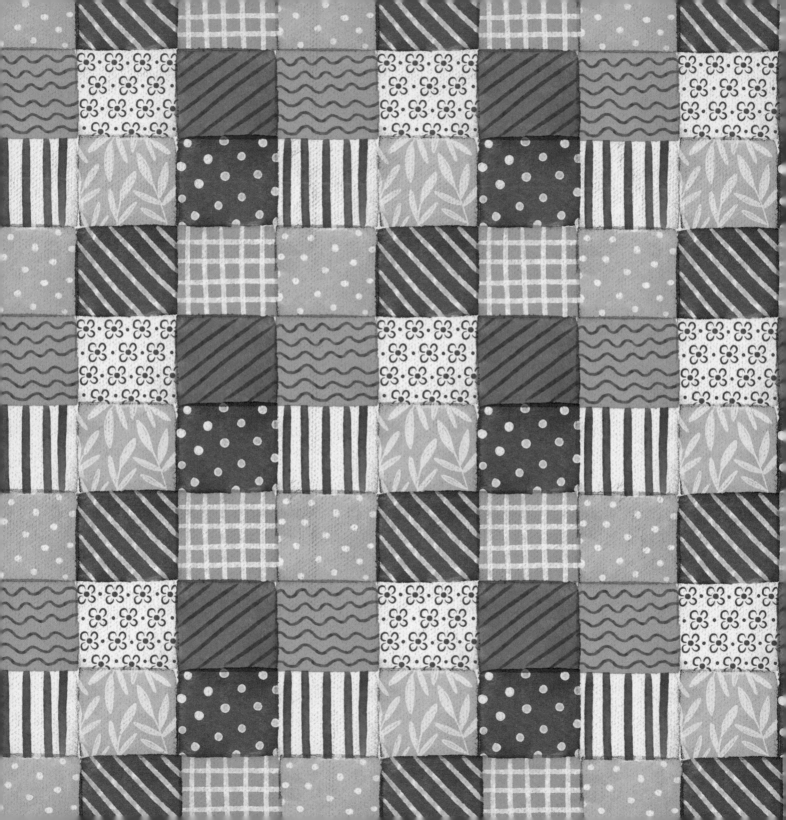